KT-528-917

For Jena.
K.W.-M.

First published in the United Kingdom in 2001 by
David Bennett Books Limited, an imprint of Chrysalis Books plc,
64 Brewery Road, London N7 9NT.

A member of **Chrysalis** Books plc

This paperback edition first published in 2003.

British Library Cataloguing-in-Publication Data:
A catalogue record for this book is available from the British Library.

ISBN 1 85602 412 1

Printed in China.

Max's
Starry Night

Ken Wilson-Max

DAVID BENNETT BOOKS

It was almost bedtime.
Max, Big Blue and Little Pink
were eating green jelly.

The sky was full of stars.
"Let's go out and
wish on a star!"
said Max.

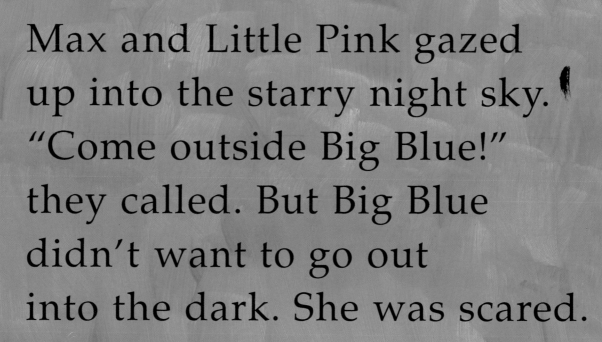

Max and Little Pink gazed
up into the starry night sky.
"Come outside Big Blue!"
they called. But Big Blue
didn't want to go out
into the dark. She was scared.

"The sky is so pretty,"
said Little Pink.
"Come on, Big Blue!"

Finally, Big Blue
crept outside.

They all held hands
and sang:

Twinkle, twinkle, little star,
How I wonder what you are.

"Make a wish!" said Max.
"I wish I wasn't scared
of the dark," sighed Big Blue.

"Whoo! Whoo!" cried an owl.
Big Blue jumped.

"Scaredy cat!"
said Little Pink.
"I'm not a scaredy
cat," said Big Blue.
"I'm a scaredy
elephant. And
I can't help it!"

In the morning, Max tried
to make Big Blue feel better.
"There are lots of nice things
in the dark… like stars…
and owls," said Max.

"Big Blue is a
scaredy cat,"
Little Pink chanted.
"I mean, scaredy *elephant!*"
Big Blue felt upset
so she went outside.

Max sat down with Little Pink and told him gently that he shouldn't tease Big Blue.

Little Pink felt sorry for hurting Big Blue's feelings and went outside to say he was sorry.

Max had an idea for making Big Blue feel better.

He went to the cupboard under the stairs and took out his special box of things. Then he went upstairs.

It was a long time before Max came back down again.

When it was almost bedtime, Max said, "I've got a surprise for both of you. Follow me."

In the bedroom there were
all kinds of colourful stars
hanging from the ceiling.
Some had long, sparkling tails.

"Now we don't have to worry about being scared of the dark," said Max.

Then they lay down
on Big Blue's bed and gazed at
the ceiling until they fell asleep.